The puppies struggled to stay on their feet as the train rocked along the tracks. Soon the doors slid open at the next stop.

"Stay where you are," Tracker told the others. "I'll sniff the platform for Rosie."

There should have been plenty of time for the beagle to get on the train again.

Unfortunately, a large group of humans crowded into the car first.

Jake, Sheena, and Fritz scooted out of their way, hiding under a seat. But when the beagle puppy tried to squeeze onto the train, the humans wouldn't let him.

"Dogs on the train?" one human said, blocking Tracker's way. "I don't think so!"

The train doors slid shut. The train pulled out of the station.

Tracker hadn't made it into the car.

ALL·AMERICAN PUPPIES

1

NEW PUP ON THE BLOCK

Susan Saunders

Illustrated by Henry Cole

AVON BOOKS

An Imprint of HarperCollins*Publishers*

Library of Congress Catalog Card Number: 00-102501
ISBN 0-06-440884-1

First Avon edition, 2001

❖

AVON TRADEMARK REG. U.S. PAT. OFF. AND IN OTHER COUNTRIES,
MARCA REGISTRADA, HECHO EN U.S.A.

Visit us on the World Wide Web!
www.harperchildrens.com

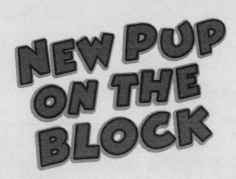

CHAPTER ONE

Jake wondered if he'd ever get out of the Buxton Animal Shelter.

The patchy-furred spaniel was adopted yesterday. So was a gray dog who slept most of the time. The big boxer had left with a family two days earlier.

What's wrong with me? Jake asked himself.

He wasn't bad looking, a mostly black Lab puppy with long legs, white feet, and a white-tipped tail that never stopped wagging.

Hey, maybe that was it. "Maybe I'd do better if I played it cool."

"Yeah, you drooled all over that last lady,"

said the bowlegged bulldog in the cage next door.

The lady had smelled good, like doughnuts. Jake thought she liked him . . . until she stuck her fingers between the bars of his cage and he'd licked them.

"Ech!" The lady had jerked her hand back and wiped it on her slacks. "Do you have anything . . . drier?" she'd said to Officer Smith.

She'd strolled away from the shelter with a fuzzy white dog tucked under her arm.

"Heads up," the bulldog growled suddenly. "Here comes a live one."

Officer Smith and a tall man with silvery hair walked slowly down the aisle. They stopped to stare at the dogs in each of the cages: a sad brown-and-white hound, a cranky blond terrier.

As they moved closer, Jake told himself, *Just take it easy. You don't have to jump around. Leave your tongue in your mouth. And keep your tail still.*

By the time the men reached him, however, Jake was yelping and wagging and bouncing off the walls of his cage.

The tall man kneeled down to take a closer look at him. He had an open face and kind brown eyes. "What's the story with the little fella?" he asked Officer Smith.

"This puppy came in a couple of weeks ago," Officer Smith replied. "We named him Jake, because a kid found him on Jacobson Avenue. He's very easygoing. . . ."

"How old is he?" The tall man smiled and reached through the bars to stroke Jake's nose—he smelled like green grass.

"About three months," Officer Smith said. "Here, Mr. Casey—I'll let him out."

Jake sprang through the open cage door.

3

He threw himself against Mr. Casey's legs, fell back, and jumped again.

"Well . . . he's friskier than I had in mind," Mr. Casey said.

Too frisky? Jake planted his rear end on the concrete floor and didn't move a muscle.

"Stay, boy. He tries to please," Officer Smith pointed out.

"Maybe some excitement would make Waldo forget about his aches and pains," Mr. Casey murmured.

Waldo?

But Officer Smith was asking, "Are you interested in any of these animals?"

Jake held his breath.

"I believe I'll take this one," Mr. Casey said, patting Jake's head.

Yes! Jake shot into the air like a small, furry rocket.

"Today's your lucky day, boy," said Officer Smith. He clipped a leash to Jake's collar as the puppy spun happily.

4

Jake barely had time to bark good-bye to the other dogs. Mr. Casey signed some papers in the office, and the adoption was complete.

"If it doesn't work out, you can always return him." Officer Smith handed Jake's leash to Mr. Casey.

It's going to work out, Jake promised himself. No way he'd end up back here.

Outside the shelter, the puppy blinked in the bright sunshine. Mr. Casey lifted him into the front seat of a van. Then he slid in himself, and started the engine.

"We're on our way home," he said to Jake.

Home. Jake felt tingly all over.

They bumped out of the parking lot and pulled onto a busy road. Jake peered through the windshield as they rolled past people and cars and buildings. Soon the soft rumble of the motor and the swaying of the van made him sleepy. His eyes slowly closed. . . .

"Here we are," said Mr. Casey over the squeak of brakes.

Jake's eyes flew open and he scrambled to his feet.

They were parked under a big tree, next to a house with a shady porch. As Mr. Casey lifted him down from the van, the puppy sniffed the air. He smelled damp earth and mown grass. A dry, dusty scent grew stronger as he pranced up the wide steps.

Mr. Casey unlocked the front door of the house and swung it open. "Waldo?" he called out, stepping into the hall.

Jake was expecting another human. He didn't hear anything for several seconds. Then a long, drawn-out "wooof" echoed through the house.

Waldo was a *dog*?

There was a click of toenails on wooden floorboards, and a low grumbling noise that didn't sound friendly.

The hairs on the back of Jake's neck stood straight up. He pressed against Mr.

Casey's right leg. . . .

"Don't worry—Waldo wouldn't hurt a flea," Mr. Casey told him. In a louder voice he added, "Come in here—I have a surprise for you."

A mountain of gray-and-white fur heaved

itself through a doorway and stopped dead in its tracks.

"Waldo, this is Jake," Mr. Casey said cheerfully. "Now you'll have some company while I'm working."

"A puppy?" said the fur mountain. "Is he kidding me?"

The old dog flopped down on his side and stared at Jake through a tangle of hair. "It's a puppy. Oh, my aching back."

Waldo the sheepdog was a complainer. Jake figured that out right away. The old dog complained about his aching back, and his sore knees, and his tender feet. He especially complained about his food—he was on a diet.

Jake was just glad to have something to eat twice a day. He was looking forward to watching TV in the living room with Mr. Casey, and he loved the soft, round pillow Mr. Casey gave him to sleep on. That night he slept better than he'd ever slept in his short life.

CHAPTER TWO

Early the next morning Mr. Casey walked Jake and Waldo to the end of Oak Street and back. He fed them their breakfasts, and ate a bowl of cereal himself.

After he washed up, he wrote J-A-K-E on the puppy's collar with a marker, and his phone number, "Just in case. I've ordered you a real tag, but it'll take a while to get here."

Then he picked up his work gloves. "I have some gardens to plant, boys. I'll unlock the dog door so you can relax outside if you want to." A low opening in the kitchen door led to a sunny backyard.

"You two have a great day." Mr. Casey

patted them both. "I'll see you at dinnertime."

He'd barely pulled out of the driveway when Jake said, "Waldo, let's play in the backyard!"

"Play? Please. My knees are killing me," Waldo muttered. "Besides, the noise makes my ears ring."

"Noise?" Jake cocked his head to one side and listened. All he heard was the chirping of sparrows.

"Anyway, you'd better stay put, because bad stuff can happen out there," Waldo went on.

"Like what?" Jake asked.

Waldo shuffled toward his own pillow in a corner of the kitchen. "You're a puppy, you'll get into trouble, a neighbor will call the animal warden . . . it would be very easy to end up at the animal shelter again," he said darkly.

The shelter. Jake shivered. But what kind of trouble could he get into in Mr. Casey's backyard?

He wasn't going to sleep the day away inside the house, that was certain. Jake pushed the dog door open with his nose and climbed through it.

Mr. Casey's backyard was dotted with flowerpots, flower beds, a barbecue, and a birdbath. A hammock hung from two trees. Still, there was more than enough room on the grass for Jake to chase his tail, even to run a little.

He was leaping toward a large yellow-and-black butterfly when the yapping began.

"Is that what Waldo meant?" Jake wondered.

The noise didn't hurt *his* ears, but it was loud and shrill and it didn't stop.

So Jake barked a couple of times himself.

A string of yips followed, "Hi, hi, hi-iy!" It was coming from beyond Mr. Casey's back fence.

The fence was too tall to jump over—Jake stood on his hind legs to measure himself against it. Then he saw that one board hung

by a single loose nail.

He scratched at the nail with his claws until it fell out. The board dropped to the ground as well. Jake peered through the opening it had left, into another backyard.

"Hey!" he barked.

"Get me out of here!" came the answer.

Jake was skinny enough to wedge himself through the hole in the fence. As he trotted under a volleyball net, past a hot tub, he barked again.

"Unlatch the pet door," the shrill voice yapped.

This pet door was set low in the back of the house—Jake stuck his nose under the latch and flipped it up.

A few seconds later, a reddish-brown shape slid neatly through the pet door. It was a dachshund puppy with long, wavy fur, and bright black eyes on a level with Jake's knees.

"I'm Sheena, and I get so bored when I'm shut in!" the puppy yapped.

Sheena shook herself and let her shiny hair fall neatly into place again. "Who are you? Where did you come from? I thought I knew everybody in the neighborhood."

"I'm Jake," the black puppy said. "Mr. Casey adopted me yesterday from the shelter."

"Mr. Casey's a nice human," Sheena said. "He brought me a rawhide bone when he planted Heather's flowers—Heather is the person I live with." She added, "But what's happened to Waldo?"

"He doesn't like to go out," Jake said.

Sheena shrugged. "He's much too grumpy to be any fun." She smoothed down the hair on one ear with a back foot. "Have you met anybody else?"

When Jake shook his head, she said, "Fritz lives right over there." Sheena nodded toward her side fence.

Lowering her voice, she added, "His mom and dad are registered guard dogs. But he's afraid of everything—runt of

the litter, I guess."

"Hey, Fritz!" she called out.

The answer was more of a whine than a bark.

"I think he could use some company," Sheena said.

She galloped straight into a large bush growing against the side fence.

"Sheena?" Jake said when she didn't reappear.

He heard a muffled, "Come on," so he edged into the bush himself. He discovered a neatly dug, dachshund-sized tunnel leading under the fence.

Jake had to work on the tunnel with his toes and his nose until it was large enough to stuff himself through. He popped up in a third yard, covered with dirt. He found Sheena standing beside a German shepherd puppy.

The puppy was taller than Jake, and twice as broad—he was built like a champion. But the puppy's expression was timid, and his

ears said something about his frame of mind: His left ear tried to stand up bravely, while his right sagged weakly to one side.

"Jake, this is Fritz . . . what are you scared of now?" Sheena asked the shepherd puppy.

Fritz's body was trembling, and he stared fearfully around.

"Puffy and Mr. Purr are on the prowl," he said in a small voice.

"Puffy and Mr. Purr are the cats from the bakery on Main Street," Sheena explained to Jake.

Afraid of cats?

Bang! The trash cans next to a garden shed suddenly went tumbling. Jake and Sheena both jumped. Fritz scuttled under a picnic table with a whimper.

"Gotcha!" two voices yowled.

A pair of huge, hairy orange cats teetered along the top rail of Fritz's fence. They bounded onto the roof of his house and away before Jake could even think about barking.

Then an outraged howl startled him again. It was followed by a scrabbling sound—a beagle puppy was clawing his way over the fence, too.

"They're supposed to be patrolling the bakery!" the beagle exclaimed when he hit the ground. "The Pearsons don't ask for much—they're the best humans in the world. And cats are born to hunt mice, right? So why won't those lazy slobs do their job? I'll catch 'em, and when I do . . ."

Before he could tear across the yard, though, Sheena yelped, "Tracker—stop for a second!"

"But I'm hot on their trail . . ."

"With *your* nose, you could track down Puffy and Mr. Purr if they'd run past here two weeks ago," Sheena declared. "So say hello to Jake—he's new."

Just touching noses with Jake told Tracker a lot. "You had kibble for breakfast. You're living with old Waldo . . . and you came from the pound," he said.

"That's amazing!" said Jake.

"It's a gift," Tracker said.

"Why don't you hang out with us, Tracker? You can't make those cats catch

mice if they don't want to," Sheena told him. "If you ask me, it's a big waste of time chasing them."

"Well . . . you've got a point," Tracker said. He added, "It's croissant day at the Main Street Bakery."

"Yum!" Sheena licked her lips. "What are we waiting for?"

CHAPTER THREE

Jake wasn't sure what a croissant was. And he remembered Waldo's warning about ending up back at the Buxton Animal Shelter if he wasn't careful.

He'd already left his own backyard behind, and Sheena's, instead of staying where he belonged. Now Sheena and Tracker were talking about going all the way to Main Street.

"Won't we get into trouble?" Jake asked, unsure.

"What kind of trouble?" Sheena said, shaking her long hair smooth again.

"Main Street is close by, and the Pearsons

love puppies," Tracker told him.

"We've done this dozens of times," Sheena added.

Fritz said nothing—the German shepherd puppy was still huddled under the picnic table, quaking.

"I'll open the gate from outside," said Tracker.

He flung himself at the fence and used the nails on his front feet to scramble up and over it.

A few seconds later, a large gate swung open near the garden shed. Tracker was waiting in the alley, wagging his tail. "All set?" he said.

Sheena skipped across the lawn to the gate. "I like the cream cheese croissants best," she said. "But the almond ones are scrumptious, too. Aren't you coming, Jake?"

What am I worried about? Jake asked himself silently. *I'm bigger than Sheena and Tracker, and they're not scared.*

He squared his shoulders and marched

straight out the gate.

"What about you, Fritz?" Tracker asked politely.

The shepherd puppy had crawled from under the table, but he hadn't moved any closer to the open gate.

"If you stay here, Fritz, and those cats come back . . . ," Sheena began.

She didn't have to finish—Fritz darted through the open gate and into the alley with the rest of them.

That first day, Jake learned how to travel from his own neighborhood to Main Street, three and a half blocks away. With Tracker in the lead, the puppies crossed two vacant lots covered with tall weeds and old tires. They cut through a minimall, dodging shopping carts and kids on skateboards. They raced across Lilac Avenue at the light and ended up at the back door of the Main Street Bakery.

Jake was almost certain he could have found it himself—a delicious smell had

hung in the air for half a mile.

"Mary, our regulars are here. And I think we have a new customer, too!" said a voice from inside the small building.

A smiling woman with yellow hair pushed open a screen door.

"It's Tracker, Sheena, little Fritz, and"— she leaned down to read the letters Mr. Casey had printed on Jake's collar—"and Jake," she said. "Welcome to Main Street Bakery, Jake. I hope you'll like our croissants as much as the other puppies do."

She handed Jake a piece of warm, flaky, buttery something that almost melted in his mouth. It was so good that Jake swallowed it without even chewing, licked his lips, wagged his tail, and barked for more.

"Another satisfied customer." Mr. Pearson was a solidly built man in a blue apron dusted with flour. He gave Jake a second piece of buttery pastry, and fed Tracker and Sheena some croissant as well.

Fritz had been lingering several yards

away. Mrs. Pearson drew him closer. "Here, Fritzie—I know how much you like cheese croissants. . . ."

Meoowwrr.

Puffy and Mr. Purr must have circled around and beat the puppies to the bakery. They were peering through the screen door with toothy grins on their orange faces.

Tracker barked sharply. Puffy arched his back and hissed like a snake. Fritz yelped and scurried behind Jake.

"Don't pay any attention to those silly cats, Fritz," Mr. Pearson said, waving his apron at Puffy and Mr. Purr.

"The big bullies," Mrs. Pearson added. And she offered the frightened shepherd puppy more croissant.

At last the Pearsons went inside. "We have a birthday cake to decorate," Mrs. Pearson said.

Tracker stayed at the bakery to keep an eye on the cats.

Jake, Sheena, and Fritz walked slowly

back to their neighborhood. They were too full of croissants to hurry, even when Jake thought he spotted Mr. Casey's van rolling toward home.

He was a little uneasy as he slipped quietly through his own dog door.

Everything was exactly as he'd left it, however.

Mr. Casey was still at work.

Waldo was stretched out on his pillow in the corner of the kitchen—he awoke in mid-snore.

"Wh-whufff," the old dog snorted, one eye winking open. "Is that you, puppy?"

"Yeah." Jake stepped onto his own pillow, his stomach bulging with croissants.

Waldo opened his other eye. "What have you been up to?" he asked, distrustful.

Jake said, "Nothing special." *Just making three new friends, that's all,* he added to himself.

Jake circled his pillow a couple of times, curled into a ball, and fell sound asleep.

CHAPTER FOUR

For several days after that, Jake waited until Mr. Casey pulled out of the driveway on his way to work.

Then he ignored Waldo's warnings, and climbed through the dog door to join the other puppies.

Jake, Sheena, Fritz, and Tracker explored the village of Buxton from one end to the other. They visited Main Street Bakery for sweet treats, or John's Deli in the minimall for a hotdog.

After his hours on the town, Jake returned to his house on Oak Street and took a long nap until Mr. Casey got home.

One fine morning the four puppies headed for the lake to bark at the water rats. They were trotting along the footpath when a big cardboard box flew through the window of a passing car.

The box bounced to a stop on the side of the road, and the car sped away.

"Maybe it's food!" Jake said, hungry as usual.

He dashed over to the box. It was taped closed.

He was trying to figure out how to open it when the box suddenly spoke. "Ouch! Nuts! What the . . ."

Jake's ears pricked forward, his lips pulled away from his sharp teeth, and his tail wagged stiffly.

"Who's in there?" he growled.

"Me!" Muffled thumps came from inside. "Do something!"

"No, don't!" Fritz whimpered. "What if it's a . . . a really mean animal? A wolf!"

"A wolf in this day and age?" Sheena

27

sniffed. "You are such a baby, Fritzie."

"A wolf wouldn't fit in that box," Tracker said, always sensible. "It doesn't smell like a wolf, either."

"What does it smell like?" Sheena asked.

"Um"—Tracker sniffed—"motor oil?" he said.

The beagle puppy grabbed hold of one corner of the box with his teeth. Jake grabbed another, and Sheena a third. They pulled as hard as they could in three directions. . . .

The box ripped apart.

The puppies tumbled backward.

A bristly gray creature rolled out of the box, snarling fiercely.

Tracker yodeled an alarm. Sheena yapped

and skittered sideways. Fritz tucked his tail between his legs and tried to hide his large body behind Sheena's low-slung one.

But Jake held his ground and took a closer look. After a couple of seconds, he barked: "Guys, it's only a puppy!"

"Duh!" the puppy said rudely. She struggled to her feet, rumpled and panting. "Where am I?"

She was taller than Tracker but shorter than Jake. Her fur was streaked with dirt, and stuck out every which way. She had one blue eye and one green one—they were both angry.

"Just what are you looking at?" the strange puppy snapped, glaring at the other four.

Then she caught sight of tall office buildings shimmering in the distance, far beyond the lake.

"Hey, what's the story?" she yelped. "I'm supposed to be over there, in the city!"

Her name was Rosie.

"My human, Sam, named me after his

mother," Rosie said. "But what I'd like to know is, how did I end up here? My head hurts—I can't think straight."

Jake, Sheena, Tracker, and Fritz looked at Rosie. Then they looked at one another.

No one wanted to tell the gray puppy that she'd been tossed from a car like a box of garbage.

Finally Jake said, "I was left by the side of a road myself. It's not your fault that—"

"What's not my fault?" Rosie growled.

"That you were stuffed into a box," said Sheena.

"That somebody in a car just . . ." Tracker's voice trailed off.

"Oh, you guys think I got thrown out? No way! Sam is crazy about me!" Rosie declared. "I . . . uh . . . must have sleepwalked into that box, and then . . . somehow . . . it ended up in recycling!"

Jake felt really bad for her—he knew how awful it was when nobody cared.

But Rosie barked, "Don't feel sorry for

me—I'll straighten this all out as soon as I get back home!"

The four Buxton puppies stared at the city, miles beyond the lake.

Fritz squeaked, "How will you do that? Get home, I mean."

"I'll walk, of course," the gray puppy said. "It's not *so* far. Just give me a few minutes, until my head clears."

"Are you hungry or anything?" Jake asked her.

"Well, I haven't eaten since"—Rosie thought—"I can't really remember when I last ate," she mumbled.

"Let's go to John's Deli," Sheena said.

John always had some day-old hotdogs he'd set aside for them. The five puppies trotted into town and headed for the minimall.

John was just opening his deli for the day.

"There are more of you this morning," he said to the puppies, sliding the front grate sideways. "This one looks like she's been through some hard times."

He leaned down to pat Rosie, who dodged his hand.

"She's bone-skinny, doesn't even have a collar," John murmured. "Interesting eyes, though. Come around back, all of you."

Jake, Sheena, Tracker, Fritz, and Rosie shared eight turkey franks—the Buxton puppies let Rosie eat two whole ones herself.

John filled a bowl with cool water for them to drink before he went inside and started working.

The puppies sat in the shade of John's truck to let the franks settle.

Rosie's eyes were closing. She slumped

over onto Jake, breathing deeply—she was asleep.

"She's worn out," Tracker said in a low voice.

"What are we going to do with her?" said Sheena. "She can't go home."

"Even if she could get home . . . ," Fritz whispered.

"They don't want her," Jake said. "I know."

There'd been a face inside the car that had left her stranded. A human had watched Rosie's box bounce to the side of the road before he'd stepped on the gas.

"He-eey . . ." Rosie awoke with a start.

"Want to come to my house?" Jake said to her.

"Just to get some rest for your trip," said Sheena before Rosie could argue.

"Well . . . that might be a good idea. But only for a day or two," Rosie said quickly. "It'll be okay for me to show up where you live?" she asked Jake.

"Sure," Jake said. "Mr. Casey is aces."

CHAPTER FIVE

Waldo the sheepdog wasn't happy about the new guest.

He started complaining the moment Rosie hopped through the dog door.

"Not acceptable!" he growled at Jake. "I will not share my space with one more puppy. Especially not a grubby stray, coated with motor oil. She smells like she's been living under a car!"

Rosie bristled. "Who put you in charge, you, you . . . giant hairball!"

Waldo turned his back on her and barked at Jake, "I'd watch my step if I were you. For someone who's only been here a

few days himself, you're really pushing it!"

"Thanks anyway, Jake." Rosie marched stiffly toward the dog door again.

Jake beat her to it.

"I don't want to sit in the house while the sun is shining, either," he said, sliding through the door first.

Once they were outside, he added, "We'll hang out in the backyard, give Waldo a chance to cool off."

But Waldo didn't cool off. He was still mumbling and grumbling when Mr. Casey got home that evening.

"She's a nice little dog," Mr. Casey said aloud as he patted Rosie. "But I can't have Waldo upsetting himself—he's not so young anymore. I'll have to think about what's the best thing to do. . . ."

That night, Rosie shared Jake's dish and his pillow.

Her nightmares kept everyone awake.

Early the next morning Mr. Casey picked up the phone in the kitchen and called

the *Buxton Bugle.*

"I'd like to place an ad in your pet section," Mr. Casey said.

Jake and Rosie stopped crunching kibble to listen.

"Okay?" Mr. Casey read from a scrap of paper, "Adopt small gray terrier mix, about two months old, intelligent, friendly. Call 555–4122, evenings after six o'clock . . . Got that? . . . Fine. Thank you."

"Harumph," Waldo rumbled from his own dish.

"I'm history," Rosie whispered to Jake.

She crept silently across the kitchen floor to the dog door and crawled through it.

Jake joined her in the backyard, and he tried to talk her into staying in Buxton.

"You could have a great life here, Rosie," he said. "I know you'd get adopted by a nice family. You'd have a good home with a big yard and plenty to eat. The five of us could hang around together all the time."

"I'm not suited to life in the middle of

nowhere," Rosie declared. "So I'm leaving right now instead of tomorrow—no big deal."

"You can't leave until you say good-bye to the other puppies," Jake told her.

They'd planned to meet Sheena, Tracker, and Fritz in the alley next to Fritz's house. Jake was hoping the dachshund or the beagle could talk some sense into Rosie.

And they tried.

"You're already here, right? It'd be so much easier to stay put," said Sheena. "Maybe you could adopt John at the deli for your human—turkey franks every day?"

"I already have a human in the city," Rosie said.

"The trip back there will be dangerous," Tracker told her. "You're just a puppy."

"You won't make it!" Fritz whined.

Rosie was firm, however.

"I'm a city pup—I belong on West 44th Street with my human," she said. "And that's where I'm going."

The puppies touched noses and wagged their tails good-bye—there was nothing more they could say.

Rosie set off down the sidewalk. She

was headed toward the lake, and the city far beyond it.

"Thanks for helping me out," she called over her shoulder.

Rosie looked so small.

The four Buxton puppies plopped down in the alley, too upset to plan how they'd spend their day.

"Rosie's not as tough as she thinks she is," Jake said after a while.

"She'll be okay," Sheena said. But she didn't sound as though she really believed it.

"I know how scary the city is," Fritz said. "I've heard Greg and Marcia talking about it."

Greg and Marcia were Fritz's humans.

"Rosie's used to the city," said Tracker. "But how will she get from here to there? She's never walked it—she rode in that car, closed up in a box. So there's no scent trail for her to follow."

"Who knows what's in between here and there?" Fritz whimpered. "Terrible stuff!"

"We could have kept her company for a

while," Jake said. "Five of us together would have been safer than one puppy on her own. Just until she got close to the city."

"But what if we couldn't have found our way home again?" Fritz said fearfully.

"I can get us back from anywhere," Tracker said to Jake.

"So . . . ," Sheena said, one ear raised.

"So let's do it!" Jake jumped to his feet. "Before she's too far ahead of us."

Sheena stood up, too, and shook her hair into place. "Ready when you are," she said.

"Not me," said Fritz. "You guys are crazy." He pressed himself flat against his gate as though he'd like to disappear. "I'm staying right here."

"Fine. Tracker, lead the way," said Sheena.

The beagle puppy lowered his head to sniff the sidewalk. "Here's Rosie's scent, sort of spicy, with a touch of motor oil— it'll be easy to follow. Just give me some room. . . ."

Tracker started down the sidewalk, beagle

nose to the concrete, with Jake and Sheena several feet behind him.

Fritz fidgeted outside his house for as long as he could stand it. Then he jumped to his feet.

He was running so fast when he caught up with the others that he crashed right into Jake and Sheena.

"Hey—watch it!" Sheena yelped.

"Are you with us?" Jake asked the shepherd puppy.

Fritz was trembling, but he wagged his tail. "Yes."

Sheena said, "Good for you, Fritzie."

"I'd be just as frightened if I stayed at home, worrying about all of you," Fritz said.

CHAPTER SIX

Rosie had headed for the lake on the straightest course she could take. She'd dodged around houses, cut through backyards, even crawled through a storm drain.

So Tracker, Jake, Sheena, and Fritz took exactly the same route across Buxton.

Humans along the way shouted at them: "Hey, you dogs! Get out of my flower beds!"

And, "Fred, Fred—why are there four little animals trotting across our front porch?"

Rosie had moved faster than the Buxton puppies would have imagined, however. By the time they reached the banks of the lake, the city puppy was nowhere in sight.

"You're sure she came this way, Tracker?" Jake asked.

"My nose has never been wrong," the beagle puppy said. "But now I'm having a hard time. . . ."

He snuffled back and forth on the shoreline, exploring with his nose.

"It's so wet and muddy and slimy and mossy here," he murmured. "There are too many smells."

Out in the water, a couple of greasy-looking rats were sunning themselves on a floating log. They nudged each other as they watched the puppies through their hard black eyes.

"Did you see another puppy around here?" Jake called out to them.

"Why should we tell you?" one of the rats replied, flicking his slick pink tail at them. "You've never done us any favors."

"Yeah, nuts to puppies!" sneered the other rat. "Nyaa, nyaa!"

Sheena growled, "Keep this up, and I'll

43

swim out there, and—"

"*You'll* swim out here?" Both rats laughed loudly.

"If all that hair got wet, it'd sink you like a stone!" the larger rat said.

"It'd pull you right down to the bottom and you'd drown!" said the other.

"But *I* wouldn't drown—I'm mostly Labrador retriever!" Jake barked at them. "I can swim circles around you, and over you and under you, too!"

Not that he'd ever swum in his life. But swimming was in his blood, Jake was sure. He waded out into the water at once.

The smaller rat said hurriedly, "Okay, okay—just kidding."

"Yeah, we saw another puppy," said the larger rat. "She went that way," and he pointed north.

Tracker moved toward the north end of the lake. He sniffed and snorted at the ground as he looked for the right scent.

"You'd better be telling us the truth!" Sheena warned the rats on the log.

"Because if you aren't . . . ," Jake showed his sharp, white teeth.

Suddenly Tracker's tail wagged so fast that it was little more than a blur.

"Here she is!" he yelped. "I've picked up Rosie's trail again."

"Do you think you scared us?" the rats shrieked as all four puppies started trotting away. "Loserssss."

Jake stopped short to growl at them.

But Sheena said, "Come on, Jake—we'll deal with them later."

Tracker moved faster and faster, with the other puppies following behind him.

They circled the lake and dashed past the last few houses in Buxton. They were farther away from their homes than they'd ever been.

Aimed straight at the far-away office buildings, they bounded across a plowed field.

"Guys, I think we should turn around," Fritz whimpered. "We're never going to catch up with Rosie."

"Shut up, Fritz," said Jake, his paws kicking

up clouds of dust with every step he took.

"Save your breath and run," said Sheena, sneezing.

But after they'd run for a mile or so, Fritz whined, "I can't see the city anymore."

That was true. The puppies were faced with what seemed to be a solid wall of trees and brush at the end of a third plowed field. Gnarled trunks and branches blocked their way, blotted out the office buildings, even covered the sun.

"I didn't know there was so much green in the world," Jake said.

"Are you sure Rosie went through there?" Sheena asked Tracker doubtfully.

"Her trail leads straight into the thicket," Tracker said.

"What if it's full of wild beasts?" Fritz wailed. "We could be . . . eaten!"

"Don't be such a chicken!" Jake barked. Maybe he was beginning to have some doubts himself.

"Nobody's big enough to eat *you*, Fritz,"

Sheena pointed out. She seemed a little less certain about her own size, however.

"Well, here goes," Tracker said, his nose twitching. He stepped forward . . . and the green swallowed him up.

Jake, Sheena, even Fritz weren't far behind.

The underbrush closed about them. It was shadowy and cool inside the woods. The puppies heard sounds that were new and strange, tappings and clickings and sighs.

"Go back! Go back!" a bird squawked from high above them.

Fritz squeaked, "Let's go back!"

"Rosie's trail is getting stronger," Tracker reported, "which means we're catching up with her."

The puppies bunched together. Closer felt safer.

They wound through the thicket, climbing over fallen tree trunks and dodging around thorny bushes, until they popped out in a small clearing.

Tracker lifted his head from the trail. "What's that smell?" he said sharply.

"I smell it, too," Jake said.

The air was filled with a dark, powerful scent that made the hairs on his shoulders stand straight up.

"So do I," said Sheena, wrinkling her nose. "A . . . huge dog?"

"A wolf!" Fritz whispered.

There was a rustling in the leaves, and a smoothly dangerous voice announced, "Actually, I'm a coyote—Claude Coyote."

A brownish-gray animal three times taller than Fritz glided into the clearing.

He smiled, revealing dozens of pointy yellow teeth.

CHAPTER SEVEN

Jake's blood turned to ice.

He'd heard all about coyotes at the animal shelter: how clever they were, how strong and swift. And especially how puppies were their favorite meal.

Jake noticed a slight bulge in the coyote's stomach.

Had he already eaten Rosie?

How long would it take him to eat *them*?

Claude Coyote was sizing them up with his glittering dark eyes. A long, red tongue stretched out—he licked his lips.

Fritz was the first to find his voice. "Run!" he shrieked.

The shepherd puppy had been last in line, so he was closest to the edge of the clearing. He fell over his own feet twice, but he finally escaped into the underbrush.

"He was a little too big for me, anyhow," Claude murmured. "But you . . ."

With a snap, yellow teeth closed on Sheena's collar!

The dachshund puppy struggled helplessly.

"Save yourselves!" she barked bravely to Jake and Tracker.

Instead, Jake hurled himself at the coyote.

He clamped down on Claude's haunch with his sharp puppy teeth. He almost choked on the bitter taste of coyote.

Tracker grabbed Claude's ankle.

"Don't make me laugh!" The coyote shook them off as if they were no more bothersome than a couple of flies. Then he mashed Tracker down on the ground with a large front paw.

"When my mate, Bonnie, returns," the

coyote said through clenched teeth, because he was still gripping Sheena's collar—"there'll be one fine fat puppy apiece."

Jake circled Claude as Sheena and Tracker howled hopelessly. How could he save his friends from a horrible death?

Then Jake heard another noise somewhere in the underbrush. Was it Claude's mate, back already?

A thundering growl echoed across the clearing!

Claude turned loose of Sheena's collar so fast that his teeth snapped together.

The dachshund puppy rolled away from him and lay still.

"Is that a bear?" the coyote muttered.

He lifted his head high to sniff the air. The paw he'd pressed down on Tracker's neck lightened a little, as he considered a retreat.

Another tremendous growl convinced Claude. The coyote sprang away from the puppies and slipped silently into the bushes.

"We're free!" Sheena panted.

"Only a bear to worry about!" Jake said grimly.

How fast were bears?

Which way should the puppies run, with two coyotes and a bear waiting to grab them?

But Tracker and Sheena couldn't run anywhere, not yet.

Tracker was still gasping for the breath that Claude had mashed out of him.

Sheena seemed too shaken to do more than stagger to her feet.

Jake braced himself for a fight to the finish—there was a smidgin of fighting blood in his veins, too. . . .

That's when a large tan and black puppy crashed into the clearing.

"Fritz!" Jake, Sheena, and Tracker all shouted at once.

"You stuck around!" said Jake.

"Wh-where's the bear?" Sheena wheezed.

"That was me," Fritz replied proudly.

"No way!" Tracker said.

"My voice went hoarse," Fritz explained. The shepherd puppy was growing up.

"Lucky for us it happened today," Sheena said.

"We've got to get out of here before Claude comes back," Jake urged.

"Or Bonnie," Tracker added.

"And go home?" Fritz whined hopefully— he wasn't entirely grown up yet.

Tracker was rolling in the leaves to rid himself of coyote stink. Now he took a deep breath and held it for a moment.

When he blew it out again, he said, "It wouldn't be safe to turn back toward home—I smell coyotes in that direction."

Jake was almost afraid to ask him if he smelled Rosie anywhere. Had the bulge in Claude's stomach really been their friend?

Tracker was snuffling along the edges of the clearing. He stopped beside a large

stump, his nose quivering, his tail wagging.

"Did you find something?" said Sheena.

"It's Rosie, all right!" Tracker reported. "Spicy, with a trace of motor oil. She headed into the trees right here. . . ."

The four puppies were off again, hurrying away from the scene of their troubles.

It wasn't long before the trees and shrubs opened up a little, sunshine streamed in. . . .

Jake, Tracker, Sheena, and Fritz burst out of the underbrush.

They found themselves standing behind a train station, on the outskirts of a new town.

CHAPTER EIGHT

"She went up there," Tracker said, his nose twitching a mile a minute. "Onto the platform."

He and the other puppies climbed some steps, to a platform right beside the train tracks. A few humans were standing at the far end, reading newspapers.

"Rosie's scent gets stronger and stronger . . . until all at once it disappears," Tracker told Jake, Sheena, and Fritz. "Which means she—"

"Rosie took a *train*?" Sheena yapped.

"Unless an eagle grabbed her," Fritz mumbled.

"Fritz!" Sheena said.

"Are you sure, Tracker?" Jake said.

"My nose never lies," said Tracker. "She was right here. And then she wasn't."

"She's long gone. Now we have to find our way back to Buxton," Fritz said.

But Jake didn't feel right just forgetting about Rosie.

"We've come this far—we've done the hard part," he said. "Why not finish what we started, and make sure Rosie really made it to the city?"

"You want to hitch a ride, too?" Sheena was beginning to look at Jake very strangely.

"I guess . . . I do," Jake said.

Why?

Because he and Rosie had shared their food twice, and they'd even shared a pillow the night before?

But they shared a lot more than that.

They were both mutts, not registered dogs like Sheena and Tracker and Fritz. Nobody had wanted either one of them,

although Rosie hadn't faced up to that yet.

Jake knew she'd need a friend more than most.

He heard a humming sound growing louder. Soon he could feel a drumming on the ground.

"Train's coming," Tracker said.

"You guys go home. I'll ride this train to the end of the tracks, see Rosie, and then I'll ride it back to Buxton," Jake told the other puppies.

The train roared into the station and stopped with a shrieking of brakes.

The doors to the last car were directly in front of the four puppies.

With a *whooosh*, the doors slid open. Jake peered into the car.

"It's empty," he told the others. "No problem."

Jake stepped carefully onto the train.

As Tracker, Sheena, and Fritz stared in at him, a voice bellowed: "All abo-o-oard!"

"I know I'll be sorry for this," Sheena

said. "But . . ." She shook her long hair smooth and followed Jake into the car.

"Thanks for coming with me!" Jake said to the dachshund puppy. "I owe you."

"Big time," said Sheena.

"You'll need my nose." Tracker jumped on the train, too.

Fritz was alone on the platform.

The train doors were sliding slowly closed.

"No!" the shepherd puppy yelped.

He hurled himself forward, and the doors shut on his plump sides. Fritz howled in terror. But the doors sprang open again, just long enough for him to lurch aboard.

The train sped away from the station.

"I can't believe I did this, I can't believe I did this," Fritz murmured over and over.

Clouds, trees, and rooftops whizzed past the windows. The puppies struggled to stay on their feet as the train rocked along the tracks.

Soon the doors slid open at the next stop.

"Stay where you are," Tracker told the others. "I'll sniff the platform for Rosie."

There should have been plenty of time for the beagle to get on the train again.

Unfortunately a large group of humans crowded into the car first.

Jake, Sheena, and Fritz scooted out of their way, hiding under a seat.

But when the beagle puppy tried to squeeze onto the train, the humans wouldn't let him.

"Dogs on the train?" one human said, blocking Tracker's way. "I don't think so!"

"I'm allergic to dog hair," said another. "Please get out of here! Go home!"

"Call the conductor!" said a third.

The train doors slid shut. The train pulled out of the station.

Tracker hadn't made it into the car.

"We've left him behind!" Sheena whispered to Jake from their hiding place under a seat.

This is all my fault! thought Jake. Out loud,

he said, "We'll jump off at the next station and follow the tracks back for him."

"But what if Tracker catches the next train to the city, looking for us?" said Sheena.

"I'm feeling dizzy," Fritz moaned. "I want to go home."

"Stop it right now!" Sheena muttered. "This is not about *you!*"

The train finally stopped, and many of the humans stood up to get off.

"We'll stay where we are until the humans have unloaded," Sheena said. "And then . . ."

And then what would they do?

But Jake, Sheena, and Fritz didn't have to make up their minds after all. The train did it for them.

When the slowest human strolled out of the car, the doors slid shut right behind him.

In a split second, the train was rocketing down the tracks again, with three puppies and the humans left on board.

"Next stop: the city!" the train voice shouted.

"Poor Tracker," Sheena murmured.

"Poor us!" whimpered Fritz.

"Do you hear something?" Jake said.

"Train? Humans? What?" Sheena snapped.

"A scratching noise, like somebody's outside this car, trying to get in," Jake said.

"Not even a greyhound could run so fast," Sheena said.

But she turned her head to one side to listen. So did Fritz.

The shepherd puppy was the first to speak. "It's coming from over there."

The three of them stuck their heads out from under the seat to look.

They saw a narrow door at the very end of the train car.

Now Sheena heard the noise, too. "It's claws, scratching at the far side of that door!" she said.

Was it Tracker?

How could it be?

CHAPTER NINE

Jake burst out from under the seat, with Sheena and Fritz at his heels.

One of the humans screamed.

Another exlaimed, "This train is full of *dogs!*"

A third human flung his newspaper at the puppies.

Jake paid no attention. He threw himself against the narrow door at the end of the train car. It didn't budge.

"It's that button," Sheena panted excitedly. "Up near the top. If we can push it in, I think the door will open."

Sheena jumped as high as she could, but

she couldn't reach the button.

When Jake jumped, the train swerved around a curve, and he missed the door altogether.

But Fritz hit the button with a large front paw on his first try. *Click!*

Jake shoved the narrow door with his shoulder.

It swung open so easily that the black-and-white puppy almost flew out of the car altogether. His front end landed on a tiny platform that was hooked to the end of the train.

"Yi-ikes!" someone yelped.

"Tracker!" Sheena yelled.

The opening door had knocked the beagle puppy to the edge of the platform. Only his claws had kept him from sliding off, onto the tracks!

Fritz leaned across Jake. His fangs hooked neatly around Tracker's collar. The strong shepherd puppy dragged the small beagle inside the train.

Jake scooted backward himself. The narrow door swung closed.

"I've never seen loose dogs on this line in all of my years of traveling!" a human complained.

"We should ask for a refund!" said another, glaring at the puppies.

Jake was so glad to have Tracker with them, safe, that he didn't glare back. He asked, "How did you . . ."

"When the train started to pull away," Tracker said, "I jumped onto the little platform."

"But you could have gone home!" Fritz said.

"There were no Rosie smells at the last station—I wanted to follow the trail to its end," said the beagle puppy.

"Weren't you afraid? This train goes so fast!" Sheena said.

"I was too busy hanging on," said Tracker. "Besides," he added, "so many smells were streaming into my nose . . . it was amazing!"

The train zoomed into a dark tunnel. When it popped into the light again, tall buildings loomed on either side of it.

Brakes screeched and the train jerked to a stop.

"We're here!" Jake barked.

"I'll pick up Rosie's trail now," Tracker said.

The doors slid open and the puppies were the first to get off: Jake, Sheena, and Fritz followed the beagle onto the platform.

How could Tracker smell Rosie with this swarm of humans rushing every which way? But the beagle dodged around legs and suitcases and shopping bags, nose to the ground.

"Yes . . . here's Rosie's scent!" he yelped at last.

That's when it happened: a human grabbed the beagle puppy by the collar, and shouted, "I've got this one!"

"I'll catch the dachshund!" another human said.

69

"Hang onto the shepherd—I'll call the dog warden on my cell phone!" said a third.

Dog warden? Dog wardens worked at animal shelters. There was no way Jake was going to a shelter again!

When a hand reached out for him, Jake bared his puppy teeth.

He saw Sheena wriggle out of her collar.

Fritz jerked away from the human who was holding onto him. The shepherd puppy crashed into the human who'd grabbed Tracker, knocking them apart.

"Run!" Jake barked. *"Run!"*

The puppies raced down a flight of stone stairs, and onto a wide sidewalk.

They ran with no thoughts about where they were headed or how they would find their way back.

They frightened a large flock of pigeons into the sky, and spun a rollerblader completely around.

"A pack of pups?" he exclaimed, grabbing onto a lamppost to keep from sprawling.

The puppies got themselves tangled up with a trio of freshly groomed Yorkies.

"You're drooling on my bow!" one of the Yorkies snarled at Jake.

"You're standing on my hair!" another snapped at Sheena.

"You're scaring me!" the third whined at Fritz.

"Get away from them, you . . . you hooligans!" cried the lady who was walking the city dogs.

"They're making my nose itch!" Tracker told his friends, "and I'm losing Rosie's scent."

"Police!" yelled the lady.

"Let's get out of here!" said Jake.

He dashed into the street. Half a dozen taxi drivers jammed on their brakes.

With Jake in the lead, the Buxton puppies crossed avenues, small parks, and big parking lots without slowing down.

They ran until Sheena yelped, "I can't go any farther!"

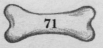

Jake turned to see her lying near a Dumpster. Her sides were heaving as she gasped for breath.

Tracker was sprawled next to her, panting.

Fritz stood beside them with his mouth open; low moans were coming out of it.

Then a gruff voice barked, "Hey! Yo! Stray pups!"

"You'd better move along. You can't set up shop here," growled another voice.

Beyond the Dumpster, a high steel gate was stretched across an alley. Two huge rottweilers were parked on the far side of it, watching them—they looked as big as horses.

"We're not strays!" Sheena yelped.

"We've all got homes!" said Jake.

"Well, this is ours, and you're trespassing," said one of the rottweilers.

"Find somewhere else to hang out," rumbled the other.

When the puppies didn't move instantly, the first rottweiler said, "You have somewhere to be, right?"

"What's your address?" said the second.

Jake noticed that the steel gate wasn't entirely closed—the rottweilers could squeeze around it if they chose to.

Luckily, the black-and-white puppy suddenly remembered something Rosie had said. *"I belong on West 44th Street with my human."*

"We're on our way to West 44th Street," he blurted out.

"So get going," a rottweiler said.

"One block straight ahead, one block right, five blocks left," said the other.

Sheena and Tracker were on their feet. They were trotting toward Jake with Fritz

close behind them before the rottweiler had finished talking.

"Not a friendly place," Sheena murmured as the four of them hurried up the street.

"Is it always dark here?" Fritz whimpered.

"It's the tall buildings," Tracker said. "They block out the sun."

It was more than that, however.

Suddenly rain started to pour down.

CHAPTER TEN

There was no trail to lead the puppies to Rosie. Tracker had lost it when they raced away from the train station.

And even if there'd been one, the rain would have made it hard to follow. The puppies were on their own.

"One block up, one block right, five blocks left . . . or was it the other way around?" Jake said, already soaked—water was streaming off the end of his nose and the tip of his tail.

"It all looks the same to me," said Sheena unhappily. Her long, wet hair was so droopy that it was dragging on the sidewalk.

On both sides of the street, five- and six-story buildings were squashed tightly together. A few spindly trees grew inside wooden cages. Pictures were tacked to them: black outlines of dogs, with red lines slashed through their bodies.

"What's that all about?" Jake wondered aloud.

"It's scary here! I want to go home!" Fritz sobbed. "We could follow our own trail back to the station."

"Uh-uh. I'm not going anywhere near those rottweilers again," said Sheena. "They make Claude Coyote look like a Chihuahua."

"Once we find Rosie, she'll take us to the train," Jake told them.

"You think that's likely to happen?" Sheena murmured, shaking her head.

But the puppies hadn't traveled far when they heard a high wailing sound over the pounding of the rain.

"Listen—that's a dog!" said Tracker.

Sheena said, "Could it be . . ."

"It's Rosie!" said Jake. "I'm sure of it."

The black-and-white puppy started running, splashing through dirty puddles as he went.

It wasn't easy to get from here to there in the city, not with so many buildings pressed together in between. The puppies changed directions half a dozen times. They stopped again and again to try to pinpoint the howling.

Finally they turned the right corner.

In the middle of a block there was an empty space piled high with smashed con-

crete and bricks. On the far side of it sat a thin gray puppy, crying as though her heart were breaking.

"Rosie!" the Buxton puppies shouted.

"Sam's gone!" Rosie howled. "Everybody's disappeared!"

The windows in the building behind her were boarded up. The entrance was padlocked shut.

If the puppies had been able to read, they would have known that the notice on it said, PROPERTY CONDEMNED.

But Rosie knew all too well what it meant.

"They're knocking my building down, just like the one next door!" she wailed. "Where's Sam? Where will I go now?"

"You're coming home with us," Jake told her.

"Home!" Fritz said happily.

Z-z-zip!

Nooses snaked around Jake's neck, and Fritz's, and Rosie's, and pulled tight!

The dog wardens had caught up with them!

A warden snared Tracker and Sheena as well.

"It's silly to struggle," the dark-haired human said. "No one's going to hurt you. We'll get you inside, out of this rain, give you some food and water . . ."

They started scooping puppies up and sticking them in a van with wire across the windows and doors.

A white-haired warden said, "Two of these animals have no collars at all." Rosie had never had a collar, and Sheena had lost

hers at the train station. "Strays. Although this long-haired one could be a dachshund."

"Could be?" Sheena growled under her breath.

"This one's collar might have had some information on it at one time, Lucy, but the rain's washed it all off." The dark-haired warden was talking about Jake—now Mr. Casey would never be able to find him.

Jake felt sick. Adopted less than a week ago, he was already homeless.

"These two have names and addresses, Adele," said the warden named Lucy.

So Tracker and Fritz would be fine.

"Why are you whimpering?" Jake rumbled at the shepherd puppy. "As soon as they call Greg and—"

"Greg and Marcia are away for two days! Mrs. Sokel from down the street was coming to feed me and put me in the house this evening," Fritz said. "I'll have to spend tonight here, and maybe tomorrow night, too!"

"That's better than the rest of your life!" Sheena snapped at him.

"But the Pearsons will come for you, Tracker," Jake said to the beagle.

Sheena added, "Hopefully they'll see the rest of us, and . . ."

"It's the bakery number on my collar, and the bakery is closed today," Tracker said. "It's always closed on Mondays."

The van pulled away from the curb and headed up the street.

Rosie hadn't spoken since they'd gotten caught.

She stared through the back window until she couldn't see her block anymore. Then she lay down and rested her head on her paws.

CHAPTER ELEVEN

The dog van threaded its way through the city. It finally bumped to a stop outside a tall building with just a few narrow windows.

"It looks like jail, only lots bigger!" Tracker murmured. He'd trotted past the Buxton jail many times, close to the Main Street Bakery.

"We're doomed!" Fritz howled.

"You are a noisy one," said Adele the warden as she opened the door to the back of the van. "Lucy—together, or separate?"

"Let's keep these puppies together if we can," said Lucy. "We don't have that many empty cages left, anyway. And maybe

together they'll calm down."

Inside the shelter, there was room after room of wall-to-wall dogs. Their cages were stacked three or four high. There was so much growling and barking and yelping and howling that Jake thought his eardrums might burst.

The wardens led the five puppies to a small, dark room at the end of a hall. They stuck Jake, Sheena, and Rosie together in one cage; Tracker and Fritz in another.

"I'll get them water and some food," Lucy said. "Why don't you call the two phone numbers that we have?"

"Right," said Adele. "And if we don't hear anything in seventy-two hours . . ."

"We'll put them up for adoption," said Lucy. "These other three can go into the computer for adoption right now."

"Oh, no!" Sheena murmured. "What if someone adopts me before Heather can find me?" Then she added, "What if Heather never finds me?"

Not one of the Buxton puppies had blamed Jake for getting them into this mess.

But Jake blamed himself. Not only had he not helped Rosie—he'd harmed Tracker, Sheena, and Fritz, his best friends.

Lucy brought them water and kibble, but no one was hungry, not even Jake. He tried to sleep, but he couldn't. He watched the hands of a clock on the far wall move around and around.

Hours passed. All of the puppies must have been dozing a little.

Suddenly Sheena sat straight up. "Someone's coming!" she said. "Are they going to take us away?"

Jake heard voices and footsteps. The door to the small room swung open. Bright lights switched on.

"He's right over here," Lucy was saying.

"Tracker? Is that you, boy?"

It was Mr. Pearson! The four Buxton puppies started barking at the same time!

"This is my beagle, all right," Mr. Pearson said, stroking Tracker's long ears through the bars of the cage. "Although I can't imagine how he ended up so far from home. And I know this shepherd!"

Fritz yelped with happiness.

"His name is Fritz," Mr. Pearson told Lucy. "He belongs to some of my best customers back home, Greg and Marcia Myers. Do you think these puppies were dognapped?"

Then Mr. Pearson glanced at the cage to the right. "And this is Sheena! Although she looks a little different when she's groomed. She's Heather Seaford's dachshund puppy . . . that's okay, girl, I'll take you, too," he added when Sheena tried to dig straight through the cage floor.

"Hey—this is Jake, Mr. Casey's dog!" said another voice.

John from John's Deli had come to the shelter with Mr. Pearson! He stuck his hand into the cage to pat Jake. "You're coming with us, Jake."

"I'm saved!" the black-and-white puppy howled, barely believing it.

Then he remembered Rosie.

The little gray puppy hadn't moved from the far corner of the cage. She'd given up altogether.

But John was leaning over to take a closer look at her.

"Mr. Pearson, I've seen this puppy, too," he said.

Mr. Pearson peered into the cage: "Do you mean Jake?"

"No, this gray one with the blue and green eyes," John said.

"Oh, she's definitely a stray," said Lucy the dog warden. "We've picked her up before."

"But I know her—she ate hotdogs at my deli in Buxton just yesterday," John said.

Lucy shrugged. "Well, she's up for adoption again," the dog warden said.

"In that case—I'll adopt her," John said.

The gray puppy sprang to her feet and squeezed around Jake and Sheena to reach the front of the cage. She stood up on her hind legs and looked straight into John's brown eyes with her own green-and-blue ones. . . .

"I'm going to call her Rosie," said John.

Who says that dogs and people can't understand each other?

CHAPTER TWELVE

So all five of the puppies were safely back in Buxton by later that evening.

"We are one lucky bunch of dogs," Jake said the next morning in the alley outside John's Deli.

He and Tracker and Sheena and Fritz had come to have a snack with Rosie at her new owner's place.

"Lucky that Mr. Pearson was at the bakery after all, making a special-order birthday cake," Tracker said.

"Lucky that he recognized the rest of us," Sheena said, "even though we weren't at our best." She shook herself and let her long,

shiny hair fall neatly into place—Heather had given her a much-needed bath.

"Almost all of the rest of us," said Jake, glancing at Rosie.

"Lucky that John was driving into the city to pick up some sausages, and gave Mr. Pearson a ride," said the gray puppy. "And lucky that I met all of you to begin with."

"Lucky that we're friends," said Fritz in his new deep voice.

"Lucky that Fritz is growing up," said Sheena.

"Any pups want another hotdog?" John called from the back door of the deli.